1,000 MILES IN 12 DAYS
PRO CYCLISTS ON TOUR DAVID HAUTZIG

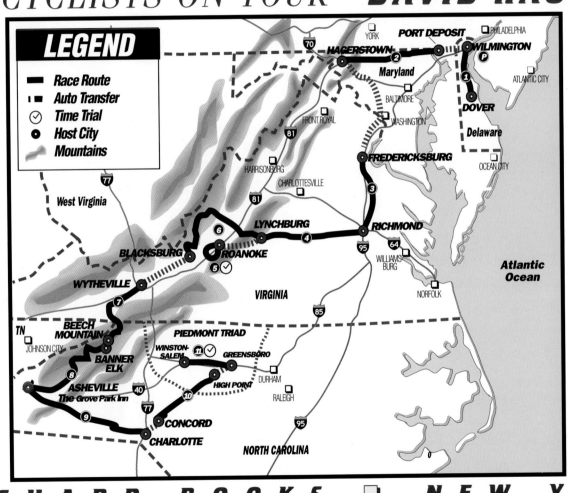

LEGEND

- ▬ Race Route
- ▪▪ Auto Transfer
- ⊘ Time Trial
- ● Host City
- Mountains

ORCHARD BOOKS ❑ NEW YORK

To a great writer, a great critic, and a great friend:
my sister, Debbie Hautzig
—D.H.

Orchard Books
95 Madison Avenue, New York, NY 10016

Manufactured in Singapore. Printed and bound by Toppan Printing Company, Inc.
BOOK DESIGN BY THE ANTLER AND BALDWIN DESIGN GROUP

10 9 8 7 6 5 4 3 2 1

The text of this book is set in 15 point ITC Fenice. The illustrations are full-color photographs.

Library of Congress Cataloging-in-Publication Data
Hautzig, David.
1,000 miles in 12 days : pro cyclists on tour / David Hautzig.
p. cm.
ISBN 0-531-06896-X. – ISBN 0-531-08746-8 (lib. bdg.)
1. Tour DuPont (Bicycle race)–Juvenile literature. [1. Tour DuPont (Bicycle race) 2. Bicycle racing.]
I. Title. II. Title: One thousand miles in 12 days.
GV1049.2. T74H38 1995 796.6'2'0973–dc20 94-33809

Imagine riding in a bicycle race for over five hours without a rest, and traveling over 100 miles. Imagine that some of those miles are over very steep mountains that most people would have trouble walking up. Imagine riding through beautiful farmland and small towns, surrounded by riders from all over the world who are wearing colorful uniforms and riding sleek, shiny bicycles. Then imagine that after you cross the finish line, you have to get ready to do it again the next day. And the next. For up to 21 days. That is what professional bicycle racers have to do when competing in a major stage race.

There are many important stage races in professional cycling, the most famous of which is the Tour de France. Every spring, one of these major races, the Tour DuPont, takes place in the United States. During 12 days of racing, more than 100 riders race across Delaware, Maryland, Virginia, and North Carolina. Each day's *stage* is from a few to over 150 miles, and riders must finish each stage to be allowed to start the next day.

Viatcheslav Ekimov, WordPerfect team leader, signs in before a stage in the 1994 Tour DuPont.

Team WordPerfect discusses strategy and gets ready for a day's racing.

Although riding a bicycle is usually done by one person on one bike, professional cycling is a team sport. Teams in cycling don't represent cities or towns as they do in baseball and hockey. They represent companies like WordPerfect, Motorola, and Chevrolet, which pay their expenses and salaries and in return get to display their name on the team's outfits. Each team has seven riders. Before the race, the team director chooses one or two as *team leaders* for the race. The rest of the riders—*domestiques*—help the team leaders try to win. *Domestique* is a French term for the "workhorse" of a team.

If the team leader has an accident, for example, it is a domestique's job to help him get back near the front of the race by letting the team leader *draft* off of him. To draft, one cyclist rides about six inches behind another, so the rider in back doesn't have to pedal as hard to maintain the same speed. The rider in front is cutting through the air for both of them. In this way, the domestiques help the team leader get back to the other riders without becoming exhausted. The team leader can concentrate on his job, winning a prize.

In the Tour DuPont, the most important prize, but not the only one, is to win the *general classification* by having the lowest time over the entire race. During the race, the leader of the general classification at the end of each stage wears a yellow jersey the next day. It's a great achievement to wear the yellow jersey, even if just for one day.

Early in the 1994 Tour, Malcolm Elliott of Team Chevrolet wore the yellow jersey. In this stage, he couldn't keep up with Ekimov and lost the jersey to him.

Like all stage races, the Tour DuPont starts with a prologue, a very short *time trial*. In a time trial, riders race against the clock for the fastest time over that day's course. The winner of the prologue wears the coveted yellow jersey for the first stage. Time trials range from 3 to about 30 miles long, and the riders go as fast as they can the whole time. Riders can easily gain or lose time because team needs and strategies don't apply. The rider and his bike simply race against the road and the clock. Riders start a time trial one minute or more apart to prevent drafting. Even if one catches up to another, they are not allowed to draft.

Greg LeMond, first American to win the Tour de France, ready to ride a time trial in the Tour DuPont.

Competitors use special equipment
in time trials, such as three-spoke wheels
or disk wheels and aerodynamic
handlebars that allow the rider to keep
his body down in a tuck position.
This special equipment helps the bike
and rider slip through the air more
smoothly and thus go faster.

After the prologue, riders face three different types of stages: flat stages, mountain stages, and more time trials. *Flat stages* are just what they sound like—flat, with no major hills to ride up and down. *Mountain stages* include many climbs of varying difficulty. The difficulty of a climb depends on how steep and long the hill is. Flat and mountain stages vary in length, but they are usually between 80 and 130 miles long.

Greg LeMond tries to gain time on Ekimov by launching a solo attack in the mountains.

Although all stages in the Tour DuPont count in the general classification, time trials and mountain stages usually determine the winner of the yellow jersey. In flat stages, team leaders can draft off their domestiques to keep or stay near the yellow jersey, or to catch up to a rider trying to get ahead of everyone else. So the standings don't change much in flat stages. Because drafting does not help much in the mountains, a cyclist can make up or lose more time.

In a day's racing, cyclists use a tremendous amount of energy, and they must eat and drink a lot. For breakfast, Team WordPerfect eats cereals with yogurt and fruit, eggs, spaghetti, and bread with cheese and ham. Riders also eat during the race at a place about midway through each stage called the *feed zone*. Helpers hold out food in bags for the riders to take as they pedal by. WordPerfect riders get small rolls with a fruity spread inside and small pastries. Cyclists carry water and energy drinks on their bicycles in 20-ounce plastic water bottles, and on a hot day they can go through six or seven of them. And in case you're wondering, cyclists do relieve themselves of all that liquid during a race. They simply pull over to the side of the road for what is called a "comfort stop."

After a stage, the riders eat a small snack before they receive a massage from the team trainer. Then comes a big dinner. The riders start with spaghetti, which has lots of carbohydrates (the starches and sugars that fuel the body during exercise). Then they have a salad, some chicken or steak, vegetables, rice, and potatoes. For dessert, they eat some pie or cake, yogurt, and fruit.

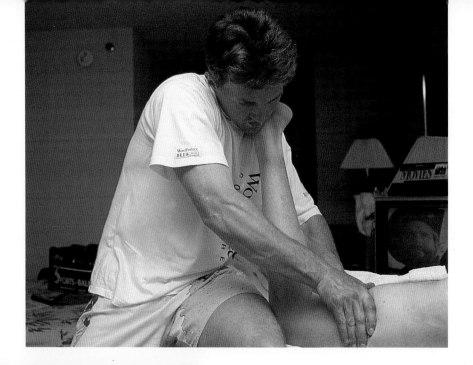

In the mountains, Ekimov holds on to his lead by staying with an attack group of riders close behind him in the general classification. Lance Armstrong of Motorola, in second place overall, leads the attack.

In each stage, the riders race to either keep or take away the yellow jersey. A cyclist who is not far behind the leader may try to *attack*, or break away from the rest of the riders. The leader's team will then try to catch the attacker by having the domestiques take turns letting the leader draft off of them. The domestiques can also catch up on their own and work to slow the attacking rider down. They try such tactics as getting in front of the attacker and slowing down, forcing him to pass if he wants to go faster. That takes energy and can make the attacking cyclist tired.

The team with the yellow jersey may also launch an attack to try to increase its lead or tire out the domestiques on opposing teams. If they tire, they won't be able to help their team leader catch the yellow jersey later in the race.

All these tactics will fail if a team's bikes and riders don't function perfectly. Each team has a car or van that travels in a caravan directly behind the riders. Team directors and a team mechanic ride in the team vehicle. Cyclists go to the team car to get fresh water or some food, to get a light rain jacket when the weather turns bad, or to go over team strategy. If a rider needs to talk to his team director or get something from him, he raises his hand. All the vehicles have two-way radios that can communicate with any other vehicle in the caravan. The race officials in the first car behind the riders see the rider and tell his team car, which speeds up to the front to help.

Mechanics carry tools, spare tires, and extra bicycles. If a rider has a flat tire, the mechanic jumps out of the team car and changes the tire in seconds. After a stage is over, the mechanics clean and lubricate every bike, checking all the tires for signs of wear and, if need be, replacing them. They may make equipment changes, such as putting a special set of gears on the bike for a stage with many mountains. The mechanics work so hard, the riders rarely see their bikes from the time a stage ends until the next one starts.

Oscar Pellicioli of the Polti team leads the pack on his way to winning King of the Mountains.

Riders compete for more than just the yellow jersey in the Tour DuPont. Some specialize in riding up steep hills or in fast sprints. So the Tour DuPont offers prizes and special jerseys to the cyclists who excel in those specialties, making exciting races within the race. One of those two races is to crown the King of the Mountains. In mountain stages, signs mark where a King of the Mountains competition begins. The first six riders to reach the top of that mountain are awarded points toward the King of the Mountains prize. Whoever has the most mountain points at the end of each stage wears the King of the Mountains jersey the next day, and the rider with the most points at the end of the Tour DuPont is the King of the Mountains.

Riders also compete to be the Sprint Leader. They *sprint*, or pedal very hard and go very fast, at certain points during the race (and at the finish line of each stage) to arrive first at a sprint sign. The first six cyclists receive sprint points. The Sprint Leader jersey is awarded in the same way as the King of the Mountains jersey. The winner of a sprint also receives bonus seconds, which improve his time in the general classification. Those bonus seconds can even change who leads the general classification.

Riders race for sprint points in the 1994 Tour, a contest eventually won by Wiebren Veenstra of the Collstrop team from Belgium.

In all stages except time trials, the riders start together in one large pack. To win sprints and stages, a cyclist must get to the front of the pack. That pack is called the *peloton*. When a rider or group of riders attacks, they break away from the peloton.

As the day goes on, the peloton can divide into groups, the largest of which is then called the peloton. Imagine that a group of several riders attacks. Behind them is a *chase group*, another group of riders trying to catch up to the attackers. For a chase group to succeed, every rider has to take turns letting the other riders draft off of him. Farther back is a large group of 75 or so riders, and behind them is the rest of the field, the ones who have fallen back. The group of 75 is the peloton.

In flat stages, the peloton rarely breaks up. Attacks and sprint races may spread the riders apart for a while. But generally the peloton stays together, the riders jostling for good position for the sprints and the finish. In a mountain stage, the peloton breaks up much more. Some riders just can't climb hills as well as others.

When the peloton crosses the finish line, every rider in it is given the same time for the stage in the general classification standings. Of course, the riders at the front of the peloton cross the finish line before the riders in the back. But because the difference is a fraction of a second, they are given the same time. If a rider attacks and finishes ahead of the peloton by a few seconds, his time shows that few seconds' difference. And he gets Sprint Leader points and bonus seconds taken off his time. Winning a stage can boost a rider's overall standing.

Oscar Pellicioli of the Italian Polti team fights for and takes a stage win in the mountains.

Ekimov wins the last day's time trial, extending his overall lead and winning the 1994 Tour.

After more than 1,000 miles in 12 days, one rider wins the Tour DuPont. His team helped him take the yellow jersey, and then protected it from opposing teams. Wearing the yellow jersey at the end of the race is the result of many hours of teamwork, and well worth it to the winners. Just finishing is an accomplishment—many riders don't.

The winners receive their prizes in a ceremony after the race. They can't celebrate too long, however. The next race is only a few weeks away. The riders will rest and then start to train. The team staff will overhaul the bikes and start to plan the logistics of the upcoming event. The riders and bicycles must be ready.

ACKNOWLEDGMENTS

Thanks are in order to the following people, who helped make this book so much fun to do—Laura Fankhauser of WordPerfect, Marty Jemison and the entire WordPerfect team, Steve Brunner and Beth Kozakewicz of Medalist Sports, Tim Blumenthal, and Leslee Schenk. A very special thanks to Joe Mikos, my good friend and assistant for the whole Tour. Four photos in this book came from his camera. He was always where I couldn't be. Credit for the three jersey photos provided by Medalist Sports goes to Monty Allen.

For more information about the Tour DuPont, contact
Medalist Sports
3228-D West Cary Street
Richmond, VA 23221
(804) 354-9934

For more information about Team WordPerfect, contact
WordPerfect, The Novell Applications Group
1555 North Technology Way
Orem, UT 84057
(801) 222-5000

To stay in touch with the latest races, read bicycling magazines, especially *Bicycling Magazine*, *Bicycle Guide*, *Velo News*, *Road Bike Action*, and *Winning*.

There are also many exciting and useful books, including

LeMond, Greg, and Kent Gordis. *Greg LeMond's Complete Book of Bicycling*. New York: Perigee Books (Putnam), 1987. General—bicycles and bicycle racing.

Abt, Samuel. *Champion: Bicycle Racing in the Age of Indurain*. Mill Valley, California: Bicycle Books, 1993. The 1991 and 1992 Tours de France.

Nye, Peter. *Hearts of Lions: The Story of American Bicycle Racing*. New York: Norton, 1988. The history of bicycle racing in the United States.